THE
MOBBIT

AN UNEXPECTED
MINECRAFT JOURNEY

BOOK 1

D1446179

ZACK ZOMBIE BOOKS

CHAPTER 1

Hi. My name is Steve.

…And I'm a Mobbit.

If you don't know what a Mobbit is, we're just like regular people, but about half their size.

And, we have a lot more hair on our feet.

Just look at your feet right now, and imagine that a cat came over and fell asleep on your feet.

That's how much hair we have, and that's just on our toes!

Mobbit's are really special.

The reason we're special is that we live in a special place called Minecraft.

I live in a small village in Minecraft called Mobbitown.

The people in Mobbitown look a little different than regular folks.

For example, I have a big, square head. And I also have big square hands and feet.

All the Mobbits in my smire do.

Now, if you don't know what a smire is, the smire is where I live. It's just like a regular village, but our houses are underground.

Kind of like where a mole lives, but with furniture.

Also, Mobbits are special because we can punch trees. We can punch, punch, punch a tree and then "Pop," the tree just falls apart.

Villagers from other places in Minecraft can't do that.

CHAPTER 2

Now, it's usually quiet around the smire. And it gets really boring sometimes.

But when my friend Gandoof comes to visit, things really get exciting.

My friend Gandoof is a witch.

And I know what you're probably thinking...

But he's a guy, and he's a witch.

I was confused too at first, because I thought only girls could be witches. But Gandoof is a dude, and he's a witch too.

How do I know he's a witch? Well, he's got magic powers, he's got a big cauldron, and he has a big nose with a mole on it.

I mean a really big nose, with a really big mole on it. Kind of looks like a potato right when you take it out of the ground.

Well, last week Gandoof came to visit me. Except this time he brought twelve really short villagers to my house.

Gandoof said that they were miners, and they lived in caves. I just called them "runts" because they were so short.

He also said they were really smart. But, they just seemed really smelly to me.

Gandoof told me that he and the runts needed my help for a secret mission. He said it was really dangerous and if I made it back, it would put some real hair on my chest.

I thought it was a great idea to get more hair on my chest. It could match the hair on my feet.

Now I was a bit scared about leaving the smire and all of my friends. But I couldn't pass up a chance to get more hair on my chest.

So, I said yes.

Gandoof was happy and he told me that he needed me because I was special.

I thought he would make me the captain, but Gandoof said that they already had a captain. His name was Thorgin. Thorgin Minecraftshield.

He was the biggest of all the runts.

Gandoof said what they really needed was a burglar. And he said that I was perfect for the job.

"Why am I perfect for the job?" I asked Gandoof.

Then I noticed when the runts got up from dinner; I was the shortest runt out of all of them.

Oh, so that's why he said I was special...

CHAPTER 3

Thorgin Minecraftshield, the captain of the runts, didn't like me very much.

I think it was because I called him the captain of the runts.

When I asked him what the mission was, he said that we were going to steal his treasure back from the evil Enderdragon.

"How are you going to do that?" I asked.

"With the help of our new burglar," he said.

Gulp! I think I already started feeling the hair growing on my chest.

We left the next morning on our quest.

It was a really long journey.

But Mobbits are designed for long walking. That's why we have such big feet.

I eventually got tired, so one of the runts let me ride with him on his pony. I had never ridden a pony before. And after smelling it I understood why.

Only, I wasn't sure if it was the pony that was really smelly or the runt I was riding with.

We finally arrived at a strange bridge.

Gandoof said that usually there were trolls guarding the bridge. But all we found were troll bones.

"What happened to the trolls?" I asked Gandoof.

"It looks like they were attacked by
Zombies," Gandoof said.

"Zombies?!!"

All of a sudden we heard,
"UURRGGHHH!!!"

Next thing you know, we were surrounded
by Zombies, and they captured all of us.

Gandoof tricked some of the Zombies
and made them think he was a Zombie

too. All he did was hunch over, and say, "UURRGGHHH," and hobble all over the place.

It worked like a charm.

Man, why didn't I think of that?

Later, while we were locked up and the Zombies were preparing us for dinner, we heard music playing outside.

Gandoof was outside playing a Zombie flute and doing a Zombie dance.

All of the Zombies ran out to see what was happening. Next thing you know, all of the Zombies joined Gandoof in doing the Zombie dance.

It was really weird.

But what the Zombies didn't know was that Gandoof tricked them into going outside right before sunrise.

So before they could get away, the sun came out and burned all of the Zombies to a crisp.

So Gandoof helped us all escape.

But before we left, we found a bunch of weapons at the troll's lair. We found a lot of iron armor, helmets, and swords.

But I found the best of all of the weapons: an enchanted diamond sword that glowed.

I decided to call it Sting, because it reminded me of a bee stinger.

…And just like a bee, though I might be small, now I'm deadly.

CHAPTER 4

The next day we made it to a place called Rivensmell.

It used to be the place where all of the elves lived. But they're all gone now.

Now the Endermen live there.

We found the king of the Endermen and told him about our quest.

He was really nice, but a bit creepy. Every time I looked at him it made me feel really dizzy.

He told us that the easiest path to get to the Enderdragon was to go through the Misty Minecraft Mountains in the Snowy Biome.

Aw man, I thought. *I didn't even bring my thermal underwear.*

Gandoof said he needed to stay behind. He said he needed to talk to the king of the Endermen about a strange, evil presence he was feeling.

He promised to catch up with us later. So, we said our goodbyes and left.

When we finally made it to the Misty Minecraft Mountains, we tried to pass through them, but a big snow storm started.

We had to get out of the storm, so we hid in a cave that we found.

Then all of sudden, while we were in the cave, we heard, "UURRGGHHH!"

We all looked at each other, and then we tried to hide. All the runts ran and hid in the big holes that were in the walls of the cave. I hid under a big rock that was there.

A big group of Zombies walked by, but they didn't see us.

"That was close," I told one of the runts.

"Too close," he said.

But, as we started walking, one of the other runts slipped and fell. Next thing we know, all of the Zombies came running back.

We tried to hide again, but there were too many of them. So, they took us prisoner, again.

But the good thing was that in all the confusion, the Zombies left me behind.

I thought it was because my Zombie acting skills were really good. But I really think it was that I so short they didn't even see me.

It's times like these that make me really glad that I'm a Mobbit.

CHAPTER 5

The Zombies took all of the runts to see the Zombie king.

He was really big, and really ugly too.

The Zombie king said that he was going to prepare a special dinner for the runts. He also said they were going to be the main course!

All of a sudden, Gandoof came out of nowhere and used his magic powers to rescue the runts.

The runts were really excited to get out, too. In fact, they were so excited, that they left me behind.

Boy, did I feel left out.

So, I wandered through the caves trying to find my own way out. And it was really dark in there.

Occasionally I heard a hissing noise really close to me, but then it went away.

I thought it might be a snake or something.

I found an old torch on the ground and
lit it with a match. As soon as I did, I saw
something shining far away from me.

When I got close to it, I found out it was a
ring.

I picked it up and a really weird feeling
came over me. It felt both weird and scary
at the same time. Kind of like when one
of my weird relatives hugs me and I don't
really want them to.

The ring was made of gold, and it had some
weird words written inside of it.

I thought maybe one of the Zombies
dropped it. But then I realized that Zombies
don't normally wear jewelry.

So I put it in my pocket, and kept on
looking for a way out of the caves.

I started hearing the hissing again, except this time it was getting closer. As I kept walking, it was getting louder and louder.

My heart started pounding in my chest.

All of a sudden, a weird green creature jumped out at me. It had a big square head, black eyes, a really long neck, no arms, and really stubby feet.

It looked really weird, so I didn't know whether to be scared or to laugh really hard.

It started hissing again.

I wasn't sure where the hissing was coming from, either. Was it hissing from its mouth or was it hissing because it ate some rabbit stew for lunch?

Rabbit stew always makes me hiss...A lot.

Then the hissing stopped, and it started talking to me.

"Where is my precious? Do you have my precious? Give me my precious!"

Now I started getting scared.

"Who are you?" I asked the creature.

"My name is Golem, and I am a creeper. I'm looking for my precious. Have you seen my precious?" he said.

I didn't know what he was talking about so I said no.

"Well, I guess I'm just going to have to blow you up," he said.

Blow me up! I didn't want to blow up, so I tried to talk him out of it.

"I did see your precious, it was in the lair of the Zombies," I said. "They have it, and they're laughing at you right now. They don't think you're tough enough to come and get it."

"Oh really? Well, I'll show them. I'll blow them all up."

Suddenly, Golem creeped away toward the lair of the Zombies.

Whew! That was close.

I didn't know if he could blow me up or not, but I didn't want to find out.

When I turned around to leave, suddenly Golem turned around too.

"I think you're trying to trick me," he said. "I think I'm going to blow you up anyway!"

I got really scared. But suddenly, I heard a weird voice whispering in my head.

"PUT ON THE RING," the voice said.

So I put the ring on my finger, hoping that it had some sort of magical powers.

And it did!

All of a sudden I was invisible and Golem the creeper couldn't see me. He stopped hissing and glowing, and instead started searching around for me.

When he couldn't find me, he got mad and finally left the cave.

I thought, *this is so cool! I could just stay invisible while I search for a way out. This way I won't have any trouble from Golem or the Zombies.*

Before I knew it, I was out of the caves, and I finally made it out of the Misty Minecraft Mountains.

CHAPTER 6

Later, I caught up to Gandoof and the runts.

Gandoof was really glad to see me. Thorgin, the captain of the runts, not so much.

The other runts were glad to see me too.

I think they're starting to like me, I thought.

When we all got up to leave, all of a sudden Gandoof froze in his tracks.

He looked really scared, kind of like I feel when I find an elephant roach in my bathtub.

"What is it, Gandoof?" I asked.

"We need to run as fast as we can!" he said.

I glanced down the hill, and there was a pack of wolves chasing us! Really big wolves, with big red eyes.

We tried to run as fast as we could, but the runts have short legs and can't run very fast.

Mobbits can run really fast, but sometimes we trip over our own feet because our feet are so big. So, as soon as I started running, I tripped and fell, and all the other runts tripped over me.

We were just a pile of runts in the middle of the valley.

Then the wolves caught up to us.

"Does anybody have any bones?" Gandoof asked.

"Bones? What do we look like, skeletons?" one of the runts said.

"Some bones would've been so helpful right now," Gandoof said.

As the wolves closed in, I pulled out Sting, my enchanted diamond sword, for one last battle before I went to the great smire in the sky.

But suddenly, out of nowhere, these giant cave bats flew over us, and swooped down and picked us all up!

Right when the giant cave bat picked me up, one of the wolves jumped at me and almost bit my big toe off.

Good thing he missed too. I don't think my toe would've tasted very good with all of that hair on it.

CHAPTER 7

The cave bats gave us a ride all the way to the Milkwood Forest Biome.

But, right before we went into the forest, Gandoof gave us bad news.

"I cannot go with you," Gandoof said. "I need to take care of something very important. You will have to finish the journey without me."

"Gandoof, please don't leave," I said.

But Gandoof said that it was really important that he leave. He said something about having to deal with a Wither Boss named So-Wrong.

I never really understand half of the things that Gandoof says, so I just said goodbye.

We entered the Milkwood Forest Biome and it was really spooky. We stuck really close together so that we wouldn't get lost.

After walking for a while, one of the runts said, "Hey, let's take a break. I'm tired."

So we all decided to camp for the night.

As we were unpacking our things, all of a sudden we heard a strange noise…

"TSK, TSK, TSK."

"What was that?!!" one of the runts asked.

"TSK, TSK, TSK."

"Whoever is doing that, stop it right now… You're creeping me out," another runt said.

I had this feeling in my gut that I needed to look up. But, man, I wished I didn't!

As soon as I looked up, I saw a hundred giant spiders crawling down to us from the trees!

"TSK, TSK, TSK. SCREEEECH!!"

All of a sudden, they started snatching the runts up one by one and wrapping them in cobwebs.

I hid under a tree, but I knew I had to do something.

So I took out Sting, my enchanted diamond sword and put on the magic ring.

"HEEYYAAAHH!" I screamed.

I started killing spiders left and right, and they dropped my runt friends. I cut the runts loose, and they took out their swords and we all started destroying the spiders.

Killing spiders was really gross. Especially when they dropped their spider eyes.

But we just kept swinging our swords until we were up to our necks in spider guts.

And as soon as the last runt got free, we ran as far away as we could from those monsters.

CHAPTER 8

Once we got away from the spiders, we ran as fast as we could to get out of the Milkwood Forest Biome.

But, next thing we know, we were stopped by a bunch of Endermen.

The last Endermen we met were nice, but these Endermen were really mean.

They stared at us and made us all dizzy. Then they teleported us to their village and locked us up in cages.

I didn't know why they did that, but I was tired of getting captured.

Just because I'm short everybody thinks that they can capture me and put me in a cage. Well, not anymore, I thought. *I'm getting out of here!*

So, I put on the magic ring and turned invisible.

I used my invisibility to steal the keys and get us all out of our cages.

Next thing we had to do was get past the Endermen guards at the front gate.

I found a bunch of barrels, so we climbed into the barrels and jumped into the river to escape.

And it worked!

Being short really does come in handy sometimes.

I guess I really am special, I thought.

CHAPTER 9

So we made it out of the Endermen lair safely and arrived at a village called Minecraft Lake Village.

The good thing was that Minecraft Lake Village was just a short distance from Lonely Mountain, where the Enderdragon lives.

The runts said that the Enderdragon took over their home in Lonely Mountain and scared all of the runts away. Now, the Enderdragon just sleeps all day and uses all of the runt's treasure as a mattress.

Now, the villagers at Minecraft Lake Village were really friendly.

Well, mostly they just walked around saying, "HURRR, HURRR."

I think it was their language. Or, they all had a really bad cold.

The villagers had really big noses too, like Gandoof.

But they didn't have a big mole on their noses, so I knew they weren't witches.

I just wonder how they eat with that big nose in the way all the time.

We met a really nice villager named Bart the Bow and Arrow Man. He was supposed to be a really good archer.

He let us stay at his house with his family. But he wasn't too happy when he found out we were going to wake up the Enderdragon.

"What if he gets mad and comes here and destroys our village?" Bart asked.

But, Thorgin Minecraftshield didn't listen to him.

So we just prepared to head out to Lonely Mountain the next day.

That night, I looked out the window and I saw a tower with a giant bow on top of it.

"What's that for?" I asked Bart the Bow and Arrow Man.

"That's the great bow that almost took down the Enderdragon," he said. "My father built it. They say that when I was a boy, and the Enderdragon attacked our village, my father was able to shoot the Enderdragon with it. He didn't kill it, but his arrow took off one of its scales. So the next time he attacks, I know just what to aim for to take him down."

"Wow," I said.

I also noticed that the bow was there, but there was no arrow.

"Hey Bart, I see the bow, but where's the arrow?" I asked him.

"There's only one left," Bart said. Then he took a huge arrow made of Obsidian off the shelf.

"Man, I would hate to get shot by that thing," I said.

"Yeah, well, if the Enderdragon ever shows his face around here, I'm going to be ready for it," he said.

CHAPTER 10

The next morning we headed out to Lonely Mountain.

When we got there, the runts asked me to go in and steal a special jewel called the "Arken Redstone" from the Enderdragon.

"Me? Why me?" I asked.

"Because you're the burglar, remember?" the runts said.

Man, what did I get myself into? I thought. And I started feeling the hair growing on my chest again.

So I snuck into the mountain.

I walked for a long time until I got to the treasure room, where the Enderdragon was supposed to be sleeping.

Gulp. Here it goes, I thought.

As soon as I walked in, I saw mountains of treasure everywhere. They had gold nuggets, gold coins, diamonds, emeralds, and lapis lazuli.

There was so much treasure that you couldn't fit it in one thousand smires!

I was scared, but I didn't see the Enderdragon. So I thought maybe he left.

So I started looking for the Arken Redstone.

This is going to take forever, I thought.

As I looked, I started playing by sliding down the mountain of gold coins and treasures that were there. At the bottom of one of the mountains of gold coins, I found a really cool gold cup.

I could use this to carry milk or water, I thought. So I decided to put it in my pouch. *No one is going to miss it with this much treasure.*

So, while I was having fun, I slid down another hill of coins, and I landed on a giant round rock.

That's a weird rock to be here, I thought.

Then the rock opened and there was a gigantic eye just looking at me.

OH MAN! IT'S THE ENDERDRAGON!!!

All of a sudden, the Enderdragon stuck out its huge head and long neck and roared really loud.

"RRROOOAARRR!!!"

The sound echoed through the chamber so loud that it almost blew out my eardrums.

I was kind of worried that I needed to go to the bathroom before. But after that roar, I didn't have to worry about bathroom problem anymore.

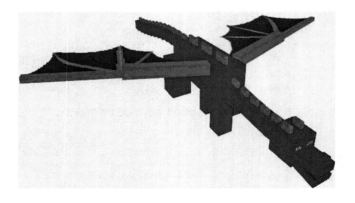

"WHO ARE YOU AND WHY ARE YOU HERE?" The Enderdragon demanded in a booming voice. "ARE YOU HERE TO STEAL MY TREASURE?"

I was really scared, so I tried to talk my way out of the situation.

"Oh... Uh... Hi, Mr. Enderdragon, sir. I just got lost and accidentally found this room and so I thought I could play a little with the cool slides you have here...He, he..."

"LIAR! THEN WHAT'S THAT IN YOUR POUCH? NOW YOU WILL PAY WITH YOUR LIFE!"

"RRROOOAARRR!!!"

Next thing I know I'm rolling down the piles of gold all the way to the bottom.

When I landed, I tried to hide behind some of the giant pillars that were there.

"I CAN SMELL YOU, YOU LITTLE THIEF!!!"

I can smell you too. Talk about dragon breath, I thought.

Then I remembered I had the ring! So I took it out and put it on.

I started to slowly sneak out of the place from where I was hiding,

"SO, YOU ARE WEARING SO-WRONG'S MAGIC RING. THAT WON'T SAVE YOU!!!"

After putting on the ring, I started getting that weird feeling all over my body again, but really strong this time.

All of a sudden, I had a vision of a giant Eye of Ender in the sky.

Then, it looked right at me!

It really freaked me out, so I took off the ring and hid behind the pillar again.

"WHERE ARE YOU, RUNT?!!!" The Enderdragon said.

I tried to stay hidden but I could feel him getting closer. Actually I could smell him getting closer. *Man, you'd think with all this treasure, he could afford some dragon mouthwash.*

All of sudden, Thorgin Minecraftshield and the other runts rushed in and started battling the Enderdragon.

They shot a bunch of arrows at him.

The Enderdragon blew out a huge blast of fire back at them.

I decided to get out of there before I got burnt to a crisp!

Then Thorgin pulled a lever and a giant cauldron dropped a ton of melted gold on the Enderdragon.

"RRROOOAARRR!!!" the Enderdragon yelled.

The Enderdragon got really mad, and shot a giant fireball and blew a hole in the roof of the cave.

Before the Enderdragon flew off, I noticed that there was a scale missing from its body.

That must be where Bart's father hit the Enderdragon, I thought.

Then it flew up and out of the mountain.

Me and the runts ran out of the mountain as fast as we could.

When we got outside we saw the Enderdragon about to take off.

"NOW I WILL TAKE MY REVENGE!" the Enderdragon yelled as it flew toward Minecraft Lake Village.

Then as it flew away I heard it say, "I AM FIRE! I AM DEATH! AND I'M GOING TO DESTROY YOU WITH MY BREATH!"

Oh no, I thought. *What are we going to do now?*

FIND OUT WHAT HAPPENS NEXT IN…

The Mobbit Book 2

Coming Soon...

LEAVE US A REVIEW

Please support us by leaving a review.
The more reviews we get the more books
we will write!

And if you really liked this book, please
tell a friend. I'm sure they will be happy
you told them about it.

CHECK OUT OUR OTHER BOOKS FROM ZACK ZOMBIE PUBLISHING

The Diary of a Minecraft Zombie Book Series

Get The Entire Series on Amazon Today!

The Ultimate Minecraft Comic Book Series

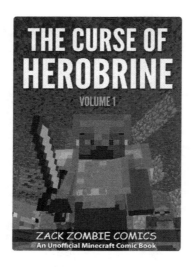

Get The Entire Series on Amazon Today!

Herobrine's Wacky Adventures

Get The Entire Series on
Amazon Today!

The Mobbit

An Unexpected Minecraft Journey

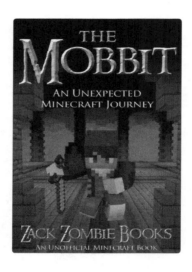

Get The Entire Series on Amazon Today!

Steve Potter and the
Endermen's Stone

Get The Entire Series on
Amazon Today!

An Interview With a
Minecraft Mob

Get The Entire Series on
Amazon Today!

Minecraft
Galaxy Wars

Get The Entire Series on Amazon Today!

Ultimate Minecraft Secrets:

An Unofficial Guide to Minecraft Tips, Tricks and Hints to Help You Master Minecraft

Get Your Copy on
Amazon Today!